THE PUZZLE PLACE™

Dear Parents,

The easy-to-read books in this series are based on The Puzzle Place™, public television's highly praised new show for children that teaches not ABC's or 123's, but "human being" lessons!

In these books, your child will learn about getting along with children from all different backgrounds, about dealing with problems, and making decisions—even when the best thing to do is not always so clear.

Filled with humor, the stories are about situations which all kids face. And best of all, kids can read them all on their own, building a sense of independence and pride.

So come along to the place where it all happens. Come along to The Puzzle Place™....

The Puzzle Place is a co-production of Lancit Media Productions, Ltd., and KCET/Los Angeles. Major funding
provided by the Corporation for Public Broadcasting and SCEcorp.

JODY AND THE BULLY

By Elizabeth Anders

Illustrated by William Langley

Based on the teleplay, "Bully for Jody,"
by Ellis Weiner and Bernardo Solano

GROSSET & DUNLAP • NEW YORK

Jody loves to wear hats.
She loves her yellow one
best of all.
It has cherries on it.

"This hat is just right
for the school picnic,"
says Jody.
So she puts it on,
and off she goes.

Uh-oh.

Here comes Joe.

Joe is a big bully.

Once he took her lunch.

Once he took her crayons.

"Nice hat," says Joe.

Then he grabs it.

"Give it back!" cries Jody.

But does Joe
give Jody the hat?
No!

He throws the hat
up into a tree.
Then he runs away.

Jody looks up at her hat.
It is too high up
for her to reach.

Jody's friends come along.

They try to help.

Leon throws his ball

at the hat.

He cannot knock

the hat down.

Julie shakes the tree.
She cannot shake
the hat down.

Skye is mad.
"How can we get back
at that bully?"
he says.

"I know.
Let's put him in a rocket
and send him off
to the moon!"

"Let's get a magic wand
and turn him into a frog!"
says Julie.

Then Julie giggles.
She knows that is silly.
But what <u>will</u> they do?

"Let's sneak up on him
and take <u>his</u> hat!"
says Ben.

"You are forgetting
one teeny-tiny thing,"
says Kiki.
"That would make <u>us</u>
bullies, too."

Kiki is right.

They do not want

to act like bullies.

Nobody likes a bully.

"Maybe I should tell
my teacher," says Jody.
"She is a grown-up.
She will know what to do."

They all march off
to tell the teacher.
And the teacher <u>does</u>
know just what to do.

She makes Joe
get the hat.
Up the tree goes Joe.
He gets Jody's hat
and throws it to her.

Then Joe looks down.
"Help!" cries Joe.
"Help! Help! Help!
Help me get down
from this tree!"

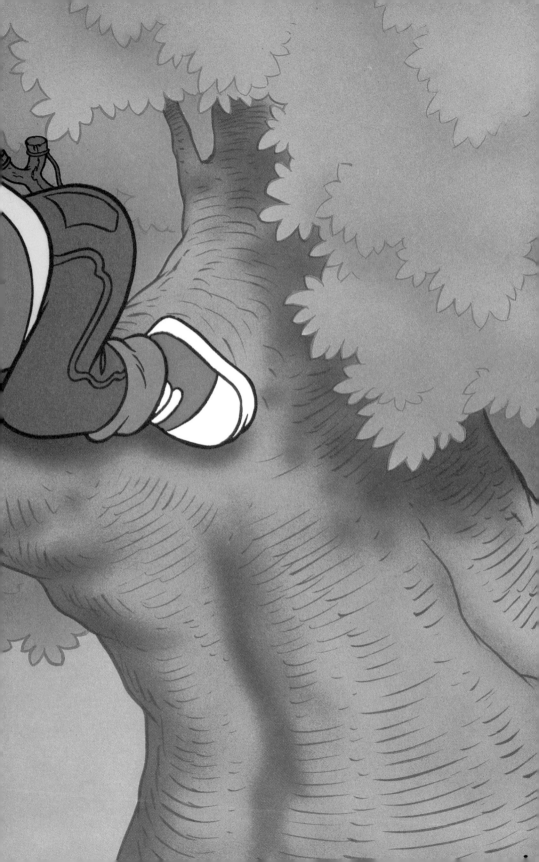

"I guess we all need
a little help sometimes,"
says Jody.
"Even bullies."
Everyone helps Joe
get down from the tree.

What does he do then?

Does he say thank you?

No!

Does he say I'm sorry?

No!

He just runs away.
He does not go
to the picnic.
But who <u>does</u> go?

Kiki, Ben, Julie,
Leon, and Skye.
And Jody in her yellow hat
with the cherries on it.